Keep Em Cummin

Tony Wilder

CONTENTS

Ladies I hope that you have a pantyliner on
because you are going to need one!
Thank you for reading!

Chapter 1 : Unplanned Encounter

It was a nice start to a Friday morning, Tre (dudes name) woke up feeling outstanding and ready for the weekend after a long work week around people he rarely gets along with. This weekend he has an outing set with him and the homies that's been long overdue. Drinking, chilling and hoping to see some sexy ladies as they venture out to the new club spot in town called The 1140 Club. Tre jumps up, says a prayer, thankful for being alive for another day, then checks his Facebook and IG. He sees no-one has inboxed him, but he has comments galore on his last post. He then calls to check his account balance and sees that OT during the last pay period paid off. After verifying the amount, he says "account balance sounds good!" After that he jumps up, turns Pandora on and goes to the 2 Pac station and Pac' s song *"I Get Around"* is on. As he prepares to shower, Tre sings along when it gets to one of his favorite parts in the song "the underground just don't stop for hoes ,I get around". After he showers,brushes his teeth and gathers what he's gonna wear, he sits down and a news broadcast catches his eyes. Another Unarmed Blackman has been murdered by the police in Louisiana... Tre takes a deep sigh and reminds himself he has to be careful tonight while he is out with the homies! So he grabs his phone and opens up Facebook and laughed at a post one of his friends made and then he posts, "Its About To be a Great Friday!! Everyone Be Safe And Be Great!!" Then He sees a Facebook friend post a picture with the profile name Pineapple and it instantly grabs his attention. So he hurried up and liked it with the "Wow" emoji face. By then his homie Ray hits his phone,Tre answers and they discuss plans for later as Tre heads out the door to hit the Bank to get cash!! Tre sees he needs to hit the carwash cause his Denali needs washing real bad. He waves at a neighbor and cranks the truck, he lets the engine warm and him and Ray finish the convo and let each other know they will holla later! Tre leaves out of the neighborhood with Ice Cube's song Today Was A Good Day bumping through his speakers. He makes it to the bank, and to his surprise his Facebook friend Pineapple is the teller at the window. He instantly goes into mack mode,but not letting her know he's interested as much as he really is! As he pulls up The teller says, "Good Morning, how may I help You?" "Tre replies "Good morning Beautiful, I would like to withdraw from my account" and gives her his account number and amount. She says "ok". Then he asked isn't your Facebook name Pineapple?" She said yes. He explained he saw her picture that morning and they are Facebook friends. And she responded yes and she had been noticing his posts also. He asked if he could inbox her and she said yes, so he pulled off and let her know to be looking for the message. Tre heads to the barbershop on West Green Ave. where he always grabs a cut from. On Fridays the barbershop is usually packed from front to back and every chair has someone in it. But today seems like Tre's lucky day because his barber Mike was just finishing a head and had no-one waiting in line. So Tre took next and hopped in the chair. The radio and Tv is on in the shop and there are various conversations going on at once as it always is. He daps his barber up and sits down and tells him to give him the usual, wave length, temple and back blend and razor line up. His barber said ok. And asked him how things were going with him. They proceed to converse through the duration of the cut about work,bills, politics,sports and so on. Then Tre's phone beeped, he checked it and it was Pineapple. She had contacted him. Tre showed a lil smirk and responded quickly. She stated that she was waiting on his message and he explained what he was doing at the moment. And she respected that.

He asked if Pineapple was her real name and she responded no lol. She said her name was Keisha, Pineapple was a nickname given to her. By this time his barber was finishing up. Tre and Keisha messaged back and forth lightening the mood and gaining info on each other. Just as Tre gets up and prepares to leave the shop, a scuffle breaks out up front. Two guys were arguing over sports and were taking things too seriously. Tre paid his Barber and slid out the door while all the barbers tried to regain order in the shop. Too much male testosterone I guess. Tre and Keisha are still messaging, she can't call because she's still at work. They both had shared valid information with and about one another and found out they knew some of the same people from around the city. Tre heads to get his truck clean and then grab something to eat and hit the mall for tonight's outing. Keisha asks what his plans are for the night and he lets her in on them, which catches him off guard. But she said cool and hoped she could bump into him. He said likewise. Tre has done all he needs to do and also stopped by the liquor store and grabbed a fifth of Crown to sip on. Now he's back home resting for tonight. He texts Ray to see if all was still a go and Ray responds Sho Nuff!! It's after five and he remembers Keisha says she gets off at five so he inboxes her, and she immediately responds. They chat for a few, exchange numbers and tell each other they will see one another at the club tonight. Tre relaxes, music blasting and he dozes off for a nap. He awakes around 9 p.m. to Ray calling and telling him to get ready cause they're going hard tonight. Tre jumps up, showers,gears up and prepares to head to the club. Tre, Ray, and Dennis, their other homie all make it to the club around the same time and it's jumping as expected. They pay at the entrance and head straight to the bar. Henn and Coke and Budwiesers is what they are drinking. The Dj is mixing Old School hip hop and R&B so the club vibe is leveled out. They are all looking and interacting with the ladies,but Tre is waiting on Keisha. More drinks, on the 3rd round now and Keisha texted that she's walking in the club. So Tre is looking for her. And as he sees her he sees she is looking sexy as ever. She also has a friend with her. They meet up and hug and all Tre is thinking is DAMN she bad! And she has a smile on her face like she hit the jackpot. She introduces her friend and vice versa for Tre. Ray accompanied her friend and Tre and Keisha stepped off to the bar for drinks. She drinks clear so he gets her what she wants. They are conversing and having a great time, dancing on songs they both feel and pouring down shots like it is a celebration. Then the DJ took it back and played "Seems Like You're Ready" by R. Kelly. And they hit the floor slow dancing real sensual. They both are staring in each other's eyes as if they want to intertwine in the other's soul. Then Keisha leans into Tre and in his ear she whispers, "I Want You". Tre was stunned, but she said it again. "I Want You". She explained that she knows it's soon but her body is telling her to let him enter her! She is grinding on him real sexy on the floor and Tre feels his dick getting rock hard as she continuously winds on him. He asked her is she sure, and she just lays a real big romantic kiss on him as the answer. So, they both ease off the floor and explain to their friends that that are about to leave. As they leave Keisha rides with Tre to his spot and she explains she doesn't do this ever, but he just really turns her on.

As Tre Drives Keisha reaches over and starts to rub his dick. As she spreads her legs and starts to rub her pussy also as if she is ready for a sexual exhibition scene. Tre drives and looks at her and tries to focus on the road. He can't believe this right now. She leans over and licks his dick print in his jeans with her tongue as if she had it in her mouth. She asked him if she could pull it out, he said yes. She pulled his dick out and kissed the head. Then she spit on it and slowly strokes it. Then she leans over licking with her tongue and places her mouth on his dick and goes down. Tre moans from excitement. Then she puts it up. They make it to Tre's house and make it in, then he puts on some R. Kelly since that's what started it all. Poured a drink and sat back. And as soon as he sat back

Keisha came over and began seducing him while slowly undressing. Tre was watching, still shocked but enjoying it as she showed her sexy body and ass that looked so soft as if it could be memory foam. Then she comes over and kneels in front of him and grabs his dick out again and commences sucking on his dick like a real professional. She was jacking and spitting and deepthroating and she was loving it. Tre grabbed her head and held it on his dick as she swallowed it and she gagged and continued to suck it. Then Tre got up and laid her on the floor as he undressed. He started by sucking her full breasts,sucking nipples and fondling her body. He smoothed his way making a trail with his tongue down to her navel. And he stopped and started licking her there as she squirms in pleasure. Then he eases down and sucks and licks her in the crease of her pelvic area at the top of her thigh. Then he moves on down to her pretty well maintenanced pussy. He takes time to tease the pussy by tracing the lips with his tongue. She squirms and moans in pleasure as he rubs the pussy and sees it's running wet with juices. Then he finds her clitoris and he spreads her lips open and starts licking back and forth with his tongue slowly at first then increasing the pace. Keisha at this moment is rubbing and sucking her breasts as Tre is pleasuring her pussy. He is fingering her as he sucks and licks her clit and she is having an overflow of juices come out of her pussy. Now she asked Tre to please fuck her, but he doesn't want to stop sucking and pleasing her pussy cause he loves to do so. But he gets up, goes and grabs a condom and when he comes back she is laying there with two fingers in her pussy fucking herself. So he watches for a second as he puts the rubber on. And then he climbs on top and slowly slides his dick in her as she takes a deep sigh of pleasure. He strokes a few times and she asks him to go deep in her pussy she wants to feel him. So he does just that and she instantly goes into an eruption cumming real hard. He long strokes her, grinds her and pounds her pussy at will. He fucks her for about twenty minutes and when he is about to cum she tells him to take it out and take the rubber off because she wants to swallow the nut. He does just that, she feels it's too soon, but she is just too sexually turned on. As he cums she drinks every drop of it. They both really enjoyed the UNPLANNED ENCOUNTER.

Chapter 2 : New Friend

I saw her and she saw me looking in her direction. She turned her head as if she didn't want me to notice that she noticed me watching her. And in today's society with all this sex trafficking going on, I don 't blame her. A woman can't show vulnerability to a stranger that's watching her. With that in mind I stopped staring and went back topicking up groceries. But I wasn't about to let her out of my sight. Mane she was a Thick One, a little taller than I, she was about 5'6 or 5'7,she had her Workout Gear on like she just left the gym or something. Short haircut rocking the natural style. I have never been with a female whose lineup was crisp as mine. But ummm with this young lady I'm gonna have to give it a try!! We both ended up in opposite checkout lines at the same time. I'm saying to myself yeah I got her. But she finished checking out before me because my cashier was as slow as ever. In my head I'm telling her to "hurry

the fuck up," because you are letting my future wife walk out the door. She exited the door and I am like damn she's gone. The cashier finally got all of my items rung up, I paid for them and headed out the door. I wasn't focused on the young lady anymore because I figured she was already gone. But to my surprise as I was walking to my car ,she was just finishing putting groceries in hers and pushing the buggy into the buggy bin. You should've seen the smile on my face. But I had to play it off, like I didn't notice her. Then she looked around, And I said "hi how are you"? She replied "I'm Blessed And You"? In my head I said and that you are, But I responded that "I am blessed also". "Thanks for asking". I asked her name and she said Carla, told her my name is Devon and it's nice to meet you Ms. Carla. And she said likewise Mr. Devon. We conversed and got to know a little more about one another to ease the vibe of us meeting like this! It was a sunny day with a slight breeze so the sun wasn't beaming down on us too hard to make it uncomfortable for us to chill and talk. And it seemed neither one of us wanted to end the conversation and leave. So I took the chance and asked if I could have her number. She said sure only if I was gonna use it. I asked how soon did she want me to do so. She smiled and said "that's up to you". I said "cool". We hugged and she got in her car and left and I was just putting my groceries in my car after all that time. My damn ice cream melted, but it was all worth it!!

First Text

I made it home and put my groceries away. It's Monday so Monday Night Football is on tonight. The Packers and Bears Are playing. Neither one is my favorite team, but I am a fan of football altogether so I'll tune in. I'm gonna cook some wings and make some rotel dip for the game time snack. I also got me some Jose that I'll mix with lemonade to sip on after I take a few shots of the tequila first. Nothing like a good stiff drink while watching football. I turn some music on, It's this artist from Alabama named Da 13th One who has some good music I've been vibing to lately. So i put on his Ep entitled "From All Angles" and just let it ride as i gather ingredients for tonight's meal. Then it hits me, I should text Carla. And so I did. I Texted her Hey Ms. Carla and she responded right back Hello Mr. Devon, as if she was waiting with the phone in her hand. And a follow up text of what took you so long, before I could even reply. And that both shocked and intrigued me right off top. I told her i was just making it home and also didn't want it to seem as if i was thirsty as you ladies say about some guys who text fast after they get a female's number. She replied that she could tell from the way I was looking at her in the store that the thirst was real anyway followed by lol. Then texted jokingly that she probably could've quenched my thirst if that was the case! I responded Oh well, lead me to the well so I can drink lol! She responded with the water splash emoji and lol. I asked what she was doing, she said relaxing and enjoying her free time of nothing to do at the moment.

She asked me the same and I told her , I was listening to music and preparing food for the game tonight. She said cool, and asked could she have some. I told her sure, and joked that since she wanted to quench my thirst I'll feed her hunger lol. She texted back, lmao! I thought damn, I'm digging her sense of humor! I asked if she was a sports fan, she said yes. But she preferred basketball over all others. I said well that kills my next question! She asked what it was? I was going to ask if you'd want to come over and watch the game with me if it's not too soon for you to feel comfortable to come over. She replied, drop the location and time!

And I did just that.. She said she would text before she leaves home to head my way. I responded with say less!! I immediately started straightening my place up more, and making sure all is clean. By that time my cuz Man Man called and asked what I was up to? I gave him the quick run down on my day and who I'd met, and he replied "mane, you always on something mane"! And I told him in my JJ Evans voice, hey what can I say lol. He told me he was gonna let me handle my biz and he would blow at me tomorrow. I told him "cool"!

Game On

I've been cleaning like it's time for monthly inspection in the projects to get the place ready for when Carla comes over. Music still flowing, the track "OHH WEE" by Da 13th One is playing now. Mane wings done, Rotel done and game almost on. She texted and told me she was en route to the crib. She lives on the same side of town so she said she will be pulling up in about 20 minutes! She asked if she should bring anything, and I told her the only thing she needs to bring with her is some good vibes! She responded that she never leaves home without them. I went in my room knocked out bout 100 pushups and 50 curls with my curl bar to beef up lol. And grabbed my Kenneth Cole Black cologne and sprayed myself down. Looked over myself in the mirror to make sure all was intact and was ready to go be a great host for the night! She texted to tell me she was outside, and I said cool. Next the doorbell rang, and mane oh my my my! When i opened the door the scent of her perfume hit me first then i had to focus because mane she was so damn astonishing!! She looked and said to me, "there goes that thirsty look again" and laughed. I told her "my bad" lol. She had on some jeans with the rips in them junts, that fit her thighs and ass to perfection! Black strap open toed heels with her toenails painted white! Black crop top hoodie with a logo that said "I Want In" on the front. That junt was fly. Red lipstick and natural face with no makeup. Mane, she was gorgeous. But I had to act like I've been around a beautiful woman before. Which I have, but every woman deserves to be admired when they are looking so admirable, Understand!!! We hugged at the door, She came in and I escorted her to the living room where we were gonna watch the game, which was already on. Aaron Rodgers was torching the Bears defense. Green Bay was only up by a touchdown though. After she sat down, I asked her if she wanted something to eat or drink right now. She looked me up and down like I was on the menu lol. Then she asked, what were her choices lol. I reminded her of what I made for the evening and the drink choices of wine, soda, or Jose and lemonade. She said she will have wings, rotel and wine and save what she had on her mind for dessert! I laughed and went in the kitchen thinking to myself, "Shid Aaron Rodgers may not be the only one scoring a touchdown tonight"!!

So I appeared With Carla's food and drink. I keep a bottle of Stella Rosa wine in the fridge in case I entertain a female guest. I've been noticing ladies on social media praising this particular brand, so I took heed and grabbed a bottle. She was tuned in to the game and was updating me on it while I was fixing her food and drink. By now it's the third quarter and the Bears and Mitch Trubisky have taken the lead and are up by 3. Exciting game so far. As I handed her the food, she said "thanks". I said "you're welcome" and returned to the kitchen to get mine and come and sit beside her. She had gotten comfortable and seemed to be enjoying herself. I am enjoying her company as well. She tastes the wings after she says a little prayer and she mentioned that the wings taste good. She asked jokingly did i buy them or cook them lol. I told her I cooked them and can cook a few other different meals. Not a chef but I can make the food taste good. Then she asked who the Artist was on the song that was playing and I told her Da 13th One.The song Was "You Gone Make Me" and she was really feeling it. She said she would have to look him up. From the music, to the game, food and drinks the vibe was on a high. We are laughing and talking shit like we've been cool forever. By this time we've taken 'bout 3 shots a piece of Jose and I'm telling her don't try to impress me and overdo it on her end. She looked and said she's good. I would not want her to think I am out to take advantage of her. She had taken her heels off about an hour ago, right after the game was done. The Packers won by a last second field goal. Had the Bears fans looking too sick. I asked her if she was comfortable and she said yes. Now another song from Da 13th One comes on called "Whine" featuring Jamaican Artist Gwap Star. And she said "ohh shit"! and she hops up and starts winding her hips in front of me as if she was from the Caribbeans! I couldn't do nothing but watch for a second as her body was moving in slow motion as the song said. I couldn't take it anymore, So I got up and joined her. Well mostly I stood still as she began winding her ass on me and mane my dick instantly started to grow. She felt my dick on her and she turned and gave me a lil look. Then she turned around facing me and put her arms on my shoulders and started grinding her pussy on my dick. At this time I grabbed that thick ass of hers, which I wanted to do all night. She then reached down and, lo' and behold grabbed and caressed my dick as it was bulging from my sweats. Then she looked me in my eyes like It's Go Time!

As Carla stared in my eyes, I stared back in hers! It seemed as if we were waiting to see who was gonna make the first move to kiss the other. The music was still playing in the background,but the vibe is as if all time had stopped and stood still. I said fuck it and went in for the kiss, and mane that felt like ot was the best move I made in the last year! Me being A person who enjoys kissing was taken by surprise at how she was a very sexy kisser herself. Carla's lips were thick and with the moisture on them from us kissing they felt soft as ever! It's like we are literally tongue wrestling with our tongues. As if one was trying to defeat the other in a kissing battle! As we were kissing, I was caressing her body and rubbing from her back down to her ass. And she was still winding to the music. I'm thinking it was because of how my dick was rock hard and pressing up against her as we stood close. She was taking advantage of the moment, which I was enjoying every part of myself!! I pulled back from kissing her lips and went in and started kissing her neck. She let out a very sexy moan. I said to myself, hey I think I hit the right spot.. I am a beast with my tongue so I started flicking it slowly on her neck and that made her grip me tighter. She moaned In my ear "Oh Devon"! That gave me motivation to keep going! But then she grabbed the bottom of my shirt and started to pull it up over my head to take it off. I didn't stop her. I held my arms up so she could take it off easier. After the shirt was off, she put her hands on my chest and started to rub,I guess this is where the pushups came in handy at. After that she leaned in and started kissing on my chest and working her tongue on my nipples! I flinched because that tickled me. She giggled and asked was I ok. And I told her yes! She rubbed her hand down my abs and Then straight in my sweats to grab my dick. Seems when she grabbed it fully she was surprised by the hardness and thickness of it from the expression on her face. She caressed it back and forth while we started to kiss again.. Then she grabbed my sweats and boxers and pulled them down. In my head all I was saying was, touchdown! When she got them down she looked at the dick as she rubbed it and said "I love that you shaved". I told her I always keep him groomed! She kneeled and looked up and asked me If she could suck my dick, I told her have your way. She licked the head with her tongue as if she was a snake, while still jacking and caressing my dick! Then she put the dick in her mouth and went deep down on my dick as if she was trying to swallow it all in one gulp. She went in without playing around And I'm loving every moment of it! She comes up off the dick and my dick is glistening from her saliva. Then she spits on the dick and caresses it to make It wetter and she puts it back in her mouth sucking an jacking it at the same damn time! If Heaven felt like this, mane where's my ticket!!

The Score

Carla Continued to suck My dick as she had no other care in the World! Spit dripping from her lips and she's gagging as she devours his dick. She stood up, and I went to grab a towel so she could clean her mouth. She apologizes for her freakiness. I told her there is nothing to be apologetic about. I enjoyed it just as you did! Then I grabbed her and proceeded to undress her, taking her crop top off and looking at her Chocolate melanated skin! And her breasts were sitting so perfect in her bra. I kissed them as they Sat Nicely In my view. Her nipples were hard and the print protruded through her lace bra. Well the moment of truth, as I'm kissing on her breasts I reach around to see if I have the luck of being able to take her bra off without looking. To my surprise I did it. Must be my lucky night. As her bra comes off and the full view of her breasts are shown, I immediately start to caress them with my hands. They were very soft. And while Caressing them I started sucking her nipples. At that time Carla starts to moan and rub my arms up and down gently

Me licking, nibbling and sucking on her nipples had to be feeling good to her because she was looking seductively at me while sucking on her bottom lip. I then started to undo her pants, and pull them down. As they were coming down her thick ass and thick thighs, she kind of did a lil shimmy to help me get them off. To my surprise, she had on no panties and mane her pussy was waxed and pretty as ever. I can tell she was ready because her juices were already running down the inside of her thighs. I gave her pussy a lil kiss while I assisted her in taking them off completely. When I stood back up I had to have her do a turnaround for me so I could get a view of her entire body. She was fine as ever! And I smacked her on her ass just to see how it shook afterwards lol. She asked me if I liked what I saw, and I told her let me show you! So we went to my room, music is still playing. The song now is "For Me" by Da 13th One". I laid her on my bed, and as she laid back I stood over her taking the view in for a sec. My dick was still rock-hard standing at attention. I grabbed her legs and spread them so I could have all access to her pretty pussy! I rubbed her pussy and just from the touch she moaned sensually. I slipped a finger in to see the warmth and wetness off her pussy. As my finger entered she moaned louder and clinched the sheets with her hands. Mane her pussy was tight and very wet! When I pulled my finger out I noticed cum on it, so I slowly fucked her with my finger with a few soft strokes and her moans intensified! While stroking slowly inside of her, I kissed her clit, and mane you would have thought I shocked her with something the way she jumped from the kiss! I pulled my finger out and it was still covered with cum. I placed it in my mouth to taste her juices, sweet to the taste buds! Then I started to lick her clit, and mane she started rubbing my head while I took my time to suck lick and kiss on her clit repeatedly! Next thing i hear is she telling me that she is about to cum, so i intensify my licking! She grabs my head as if telling me to not move from that spot. To keep licking until she climaxes. All i hear is her panting and repeating, I'm about to cum, I'm about to cum , I'm about to cum,and then she came. And a very strong one. It sent trembles through her body, and she convulsed as if that nut was really needed for Relief!!

Hellua Night

I got up and grabbed a condom from my dresser drawer, and was about to put it on, then she asked could she assist. She grabbed it, put it in her mouth and put it on my dick with her mouth. She is a GREAT one with her mouthpiece! She told me she wanted me to hit her from the back, with all that ass it would be my pleasure! She got on her knees on the bed. I stood behind her admiring that ass and how it spread. Her pussy poked out as she was bent over waiting for me to enter her. I started rubbing my dick up and down her slit and the wetness made it easy for me to slide in her pussy...slowly!

When my dick was in her she said "Ohh My Gawd", and gripped my dick tightly with her pussy muscles as if she were about to cum again. And to my surprise, that is exactly what she was about to do! I Slowly backed out and saw cum on the condom, then back in and she told me to stay in and hold my dick deep in her because she was about to cum again! And I did and she started cumming again, pussy gripping my dick, she grips the sheets, and moaning sounding very sexy!

And I am telling her to cum for me as I hold my dick deep in her and she is winding on my dick. She then cums and as she cums

I simultaneously start to stroke her pussy once again, slowly! She said "damn"! All I'm thinking to myself is "mane you better not cum right now". Pussy good and she's moaning getting me into it is a recipe for a nut on my behalf. But I continue to fuck her. I speed up with my pumps and now I'm pounding the pussy, and all she is saying is "yes,yes,yes, fuck me Devon fuck me Devon" And that I do. I fuck her til my sock is trying to slide off of my foot from trying to get a grip, because she is throwing that as back also. While still fucking her, I look down and I spit on her asshole. Yeah, you know what's next. While fucking her, I ease my thumb in her butt, and

mane its like I opened a cum portal, she instantly started to cum again. At this point I'm Surprised that I haven't bust off everywhere. I try to take my thumb out of her ass and she tells me to leave it there. Well ok then. I'd say about ten more strokes, and it was my time to shoot my nut. I got faster and harder with my strokes and she knew then I was about to cum. I said I'm about to cum, and she said told me to cum for her and fuck her harder while I do so...So

I'm beating the pussy up, and its getting better with each stroke. I started to cum and I started to tremble and grunt and she gripped her pussy tight on my dick as if she wanted to pull all of it out of me. I asked her. What are you trying to do to me? After I nutted we both laid flat on the bed and within a few moments we both were passed out!! Was A Helluva Night With My New Friend!!

Chapter 3 Part 1 : First Sight

I never knew jazz night would bring this many sexy ladies and well dressed brothers out, but hey I'm glad it did! Things are flowing with a great vibe, and everyone is looking The part. The Black Excellence that's needed to make a night like this be as great as it is turning out to be! It seemed my dream would never unfold for me that I would be apart of having a Successful Club downtown in the city I grew up in! With the help of Joe my Business partner and with our dedication to making this dream into a reality! Many trials came up but we stayed the course and made it all happen. Tonight The Band "6 Piece" is playing some soothing Jazz Tunes, some old classics And some of their original songs! The waitresses are making sure the customers have their drinks and food they order in proper timing. We pride ourselves on making sure our customers are well taken care of! At this point I am standing at the door greeting some of the customers walking into the club as I normally do throughout our nights we are open. Joe is making sure the sound system Is up to par, so we will have no complaints on how the music is sounding as it's coming from the speakers! With him on the job we have no worries because he is a expert sound man and musician. I look up and I see Joe and he Is walking towards me and on his face seems to be a look of concern. I ask him bro whats wrong as I shake his hand. He said bro, I'm just stunned to see how many people are steady coming In.

And he said I guess since we made our promotional advertisement change it grabbed the attention of more people. I told him yeah, that's something we needed to do. And we need to keep applying promotional pressure to keep the crowd like this. He said I can dig It! I asked was the band all good and he said yeah, they are ready to play til the doors close. I said, with this packed house they know money is really made tonight. We Both Laughed, then he walked off to go scower the room and to make sure everything is ok!. At this time 2 couples are coming in through the door, and I greet them welcoming them to the club. I remember seeing their faces from Previous nights at the club.. One of the ladies said it looks like a packed house tonight, and I told her, yes it is, and we are looking forward to more nights like this! She just smiled as her and her companion walked on in. I was about to leave from the door when I looked up to see a lady walking towards the door Alone. So I waited to greet her before I walked away from the entrance. She had a sway in her walk that would make one want to ask where did she learn to walk like that! She made it to the door and after security checked her bag I greeted her and told her welcome to Club Jazz Land "Where The Music Soothes You,While You Let The Drinks Use You". She said thanks, and she let me knew that it was her first time coming to the club and she hopes to have a great night. I told her thanks for choosing to come here tonight, I introduced myself as Tony, one of the club owners and told her that I will definitely make sure her night is enjoyable while she was here! She said wow thanks, and she told me her name Was Tammy! After that She made her way in the Club. Big T. my security guard,said boss seems like you wanted shoot your shot at her and he laughed. I told him mane I'm going in for the layup on this one.

Chapter 3 Part 2 : Drinks On Me

I walked back in the club and went straight to the bar and asked the bartenders Casey, Benny and Meka how everything was flowing.They all said it's a very busy night, but they wouldn't have it any other way, because everyone is tipping. Meka was the most requested bartender because of her ability to "mix the hell out of drinks". At least that's the line all the customers tend to use to describe her drink mixing ability. Casey was our flirtatious bartender, she kept all the single guys entertained as they sat and drank at the bar. Her customer service skills were A1. And Benny was the one that held everything down in the middle.That guy presence so the male customers wouldn't get too rowdy towards the ladies working with him. I then made mention to Meka that I needed her to take care of a special customer for me tonight. That whatever she orders I need her to fix the drink, but not to make them too strong, have them just right. She smiled and said, "I got you boss". "You must be trying to take something home?" She said while laughing. I replied, "just trying to get to know her at this point." I had her pour me a shot of Jose, I knocked that back and headed across the club to check on Tammy. As I am walking through the club, I see the dance floor has a nice crowd and customers are at their tables dancing to the music as the band is in the middle of playing a Song By Dizzy Gillespie. And they were sounding damn good! One of the male customers stopped me and said, "man I am really enjoying myself tonight." "Whatever it is that you all have done to get the atmosphere like this, keep it up." I told him, "I appreciate that and we are gonna work on keeping things this way!" I patted him on his shoulder and moved on. I saw Joe over by the band and he was about to grab his horn and join in on playing. He is a music teacher by day so music is his Love! Then I spotted Tammy, with her sexy self sitting alone. I made sure to have the nearest waitress take note of who she is to make sure Meka makes her drinks and she is not charged for anything. I then approached Tammy and asked her was she enjoying herself so far? She responded by saying she was indeed having a great time, outside of being here alone! I told her in my Micheal Jackson voice "You are not alone, I am here with you" And we both laughed real hard. She asked "how are you here with me you have to work?" I told her "I can multitask." It's against house rules to fraternize with customers for too long. So I am just going to have to discipline myself for this. She ordered another drink and as the waitress brought it to her, she pulled out money to pay for the drink and the waitress told her it was already taken care of. She looked at me and I told her, "Didn't I say I was gonna take care of you tonight?' She smiled and put her money up. I asked her what her relationship status was, and she said though she's single, she has a friend who she goes out with every now and then. In my mind, I said she's fucking.Out loud I said "ok cool." She then said, "I already know you have a flock of females on your team." I jokingly told her "I have a good three that stay suited up and ready to play." She gave me that "I know you're lying, but I can believe it" look.

I told her I was just kidding, and my situation is similar to hers! She said ok. At this time I had to get up and go address the crowd. So I excused myself and let her know I'd be back around to see her. The band was still playing, and Joe was killin it on the horn! I grabbed the mic and the band brought the tempo down to a smooth low groove. I asked if everyone was enjoying themselves, and the crowd said yes! And one female customer yelled "gone and sang then", followed by laughter from her and everyone else! I told her "If I do it would be only to serenade you!" That brought Ohhs,

Ahhs and Ok's from the crowd. I thanked them for coming out, and informed them on what to expect in the future and turned it back over to the band! The Band didn't miss a beat and they kept things rolling when they started back up. I walked back towards where Tammy was sitting, she said I see you mister, you can serenade me, I told her oh it's coming!!

Chapter 3 Part 3 : Last Call

The night had been going great. So great that we stayed open an extra hour. We also announced that during that hour we would be offering an open bar. It seemed as if that idea went over well with the customers, because the bar became crowded all at once. By this time in the midst of working the club, I had gotten a chance to have a nice conversation and interaction with Tammy! I found out she was a beautician and she owned a hair salon on the Northside of
town. From the looks of it she was clearly enjoying herself. She danced to a few songs and she was definitely digging the drinks lol. I walked over to her table and she mentioned that she was going to be leaving in the next ten 10 minutes. Making my voice even deeper than what it already is I said "Oh, so you're gonna leave me?" From the quick breath and momentary entranced look in her eyes I knew I'd made the desired effect. However, she still said "yes i am"
with a laugh. She then pulled out one of her business cards and gave it to me. And she said "if you keep this with you, i won't be far away at all." Glancing at the card I held in my hand I noticed it had her phone number on it, that's what she was referring to! I told her I would definitely keep it close and make it useful. Then she

gets up to leave and I walk with her towards the door. Walking behind her so i can take in the view of how sexy she was from behind. And she was walking like she knew I was watching. Like every time she took a step her ass was in its own zone, and her walk seemed as if it needed a theme song to it. She turned and asked me if I liked what I saw and I said "yes I do." We made it to the club exit and we hugged. I told her to be safe and asked Big T the security guard to escort her to her car for me. He nodded his head and said "gotcha boss man." As they walked off I turned around and headed back inside the club. It was time to get everything set for closing tonight. I walked up on Joe and told him that he did a great job tonight with the band and made sure the crowd was entertained all night. He looked and said "well thank you kindly my brother." He then proceeded to tell me that he saw how I was tryna work and skirt chase all night, and we both laughed. It's only a few remaining customers left inside and The band is starting to wrap it up. Meka, Casey And Ben are getting the bar in order. Joe and I are walking around letting everyone know how we appreciate the hard work and effort to make the night successful, and without teamwork it wouldn't have been possible. We do our nightly tallies, pay everyone and make sure we get the club clean and secure everything before we leave. It's 3 a.m. and I know it's late, but something is telling me to text Tammy. I am thinking maybe she's asleep because she was feeling those drinks. I texted and told her who I was in the text and I hope she made it home safely. She responded with "hi", and let me know she made it home safely. I said "cool." I told her I didn't want to hold her up since it was so late or early in the morning to be exact. Her reply was "no

you're good." She said she was just getting out of the shower and settling in. I typed "oh, ok." Feeling myself a bit I then added "Well, looks like I've got perfect texting timing" "Yeah.she said. "You pressed send at a good moment." She asked what I was about to do. I told her that I was about to head home to try to rest a little for tomorrow/later today. She said "cool, be safe and no texting and driving." I responded "Thank you and have a Good Night." She responded the same to you. Traffic was light, so it wouldn't take me long to make it home. When I made it to the house I parked, and grabbed my pistol as I normally do. My neighborhood is cool but I

never want to get caught slipping by someone that would attempt to rob me. I unlocked the front door, walked in closed and locked it behind me. And as soon as i put my keys and phone down on the coffee table I sat down on my couch and passed out!

Chapter 3 Part 4 : Day Time

I was awakened by my phone ringing. I grabbed it to see who it was and it was Joe on the other end. "Hello" I answered with the sound of sleep heavy in my voice."Good Morning bro" he replied and said "wake up mane, you shouldn't be trying to hang out all night." I Told him "bro hell i was with you at the club." "I'm still on the couch in all my clothes from last night." I looked at the time on my phone and It was 9 a.m. I never usually sleep this late no matter how long I am up the night before. He then mentioned that he was calling because of all the great feedback the club was getting on our social media accounts. I put him on speakerphone, and began logging into my various accounts while he was talking and I saw how everyone was posting about how they had a great time. There were videos of the band and all!! That woke me right on up. I told him I was checking it out as he was telling me. And told him let's keep pushing forward and keep this momentum and energy up. He said "fasho." And then told me to hit him up when I got on up for the day. After I hung up, I saw that I had ten missed text messages and two

missed calls. The main text that stood out was a text from Tammy. I opened it and she said "Good Morning, Hope you made it home safe and Hope You Have A Great Day!" That gave me a boost as well so I responded "Good Morning, I did make it safely and thanks for checking. You have a great day also!" Then I checked other texts and calls, got up, said a quick prayer and started to go freshen up. In the meantime I turned the tv on and Sportscenter was on, as always on my tv. I went and hopped in the shower, and as I was getting out my phone rang. It was Naomi. She's a female that I am cool with. We go on dinner outings at times when we have free time and get together and fuck one another brains out when we feel the need to do so. I answered and she said "what's up dude?" I responded " whats up lady?" She said "I see the club did great last night." I told her "yes it did." "it had to because of the owners who run it." We

both laughed. We conversed back and forth about the club, her job and other things that's going on. We were on the phone for about fifteen minutes or so when she asked what I was doing. I told her I was just getting out of the shower. She said "lemme see." We switched over to facetime and I showed her the dick while I was standing there naked. She kissed the phone screen and I laughed at her silly ass. She told me she needed a quickie on her lunch break and I told her to come get it, I would be home. She said "bet", she would be on her way when she takes lunch in ten minutes. Then we hung up. I grabbed some gym shorts and slid them on, no need for boxers because i would be right back naked soon.Then Tammy texted and asked what was I up to, I told her getting myself together at the moment, just finished showering and about to get on social media to thank the customers from last night for coming out. She said cool, she told me she was at her shop, and it was a slow morning so far. I said ok. She told me she was just texting, and I told her I would definitely get back with her in about an hour or so so we could

see when we would get the chance to see one another again. She responded "please do that." I responded "later." Sportscenter is blaring on the T.V. and Steven A Smith is going on one of his rants towards Max Kellerman about the Cowboys' game. And you know how he hates the Cowboys. I hear a knock at the door, and I check my ring doorbell camera and its Naomi. I opened the door and she said "what up dude" and again I said "What up lady" and we both laughed. After a quick hug she said "no talking you know what time it is". She started taking her clothes off at the door. She had a skirt suit on,her work attire. We headed towards my room, and when we made it there she was completely naked and laughing talking bout come on dude. She left a trail of her clothes from the front door to the bedroom. I had on nothing but my gym shorts and Nike slides, so I pulled the gym shorts off quickly!

Chapter 3 Part 5 : Quickie

My dick was hard already. It was getting hard as I was walking behind Naomi's fine ass as she was taking her clothes off as she headed to the room.My dick always does that when Naomi and I get together. I feel my body is aware that when she and I get together we will have a great fucking session! I approached her and she grabbed my dick and started rubbing it, and told me to bring that mf on. Then we kissed as we looked into each other's eyes.The kiss is very passionate, she loves to use her tongue to lick slowly around my lips and to put my bottom lip in her mouth and suck on it softly. As she does that she is still slowly stroking my rock hard dick with her hand. While I am caressing and squeezing her breast, her nipples are hard and erect.So I take my tongue and begin to lick in circular motion around her nipple. She moans at the touch of my tongue on her nipple. And her hand is still firmly grasping and stroking my dick. I stand up straight and look down at her hand on my dick. She spits on my dick and continues to stroke it.Then she pushes me on the bed and puts the dick in her mouth! She gives the best head because she loves to suck dick. But since today is a quickie day, I know it won't be time for her to suck my dick as good as she normally does.But she is pulling, spiting and slurping on my dick. It's sounding as if she is trying to choke herself with it as she's gagging while taking the dick all in her mouth. I am telling her to suck this dick,then I grab her head and she lets me fuck her mouth! And she is also playing in her pussy as I am fucking her in her mouth. I love the freakiness about her. Her mouth is so wet and saliva is dripping from her mouth as my dick goes in and out.Then I go in slow and deep until she gags, she loves that shit. And I DO TOO! To see her transform from her corporate attire to this dick sucking beauty in a matter of minutes is amazing. I pull my dick out and tell her, "you know we don't have long." She says"you're right,

so come on and fuck me!" Then she says no, she wanted to ride the dick. So as I lay on the bed, she climbs on top. Her pussy is so wet, even before she puts my dick in, her juices start dripping on my dick head. Then she slides it in real slow. She lets out a deep sigh and a moan as my dick enters her wet and warm pussy. She slowly goes all the way down on my dick and grips it with her pussy muscles. And she comes back to the top and slowly goes down all the while still gripping my dick tight with her wet and hot pussy.I am holding both of her breasts as she is riding my dick. She's moaning and I'm moaning too! We are both caught up in the moments of this sexual pleasure. She goes down and starts to grind with my dick deep inside of her. While she grinds I start to thrust my dick in her and she moans and says fuck yeah! I then sit up and I cuff my arms under hers and grab her shoulders and begin to pull her down on my

dick while pushing the dick inside of her at the same time. We are both panting as if we are in a race of some sort. We are both trying to get these nuts because she has to get back to work. Then I lie back down and she just goes to work riding my dick. Up and down, back and forth, and grinding until she tells me she's about to cum. She speeds up riding and she moans louder and say oh fuck

I'm cumming, Then she says it again and suddenly she starts to shake and as she shakes I myself am about to cum. I tell her I am about to cum, she gets off my dick and sticks it in her mouth, and starts to suck and jack my dick to help me cum. I tell her "here it comes" and she says "give it to me", then I can only say "shittttt!" I start to cum and she catches it and jacks my dick to make sure all she gets every drop of cum out of it. She sucks and pulls as if she's trying to empty my body of cum. She spits some cum back on my dick and she slurps

it right back up. And all I could say is "oh my goodness." She said "I see you're still eating healthy." I told her "yeah so you can keep drinking this healthy nut." She then jumps up, goes to

shower,puts her clothes on and heads to work!

Chapter 3 Part 6 : Play Your Role 1

It's now about one in the afternoon and I finally call Joe back. He said he was checking on some sound system features.I told him ok and let him know I was about to head that way. We hung up and I had to shower and freshen up again from the mid day sex session. I'm completely relaxed and laid back and I could really lay down and take a nap, but it's time for business. I had already played enough. The television still blaring in the background, with Sage Steele's sexy ass doing her sports segment. She is looking beautiful today, and I'm thinking mane she can showl get it. Now that I'm all freshened up, I grab my pistol, keys and say another quick prayer before I head out of the door. I always acknowledge the fact that I need a higher power to protect me in my daily routine in life, because it is a crazy world out here. I walk outside and my neighbor John is in his front yard. We speak to one another and he mentions something about a game that was on last night. We have a brief exchange about it, then I hop in the car and crank it up and let it warm for a second. I flipped my radio on, and I still had the Da 13th One, this artist from Alabama album playing. The song "Anything Is Possible Is On", a great song for some midday motivation! As I left heading to the club, I called Tammy. I asked her what she was doing. She said she had three clients in the shop and was almost done with two of them. I said to her cool. Get that money. She asked what were my plans for tonight? I told her I was going to be at the club, she said ok. I told her if she wasn't busy to come by and have a few drinks. She said she would do just that. We hung up as I was just pulling up to the club. I parked in my designated spot, got out and walked in. I see Joe up at the stage area and I see Meka over behind the bar straightening things. I walked over to greet and hug her, and asked her if she was ready to get people drunk today. "That's what I'm here for!" she replied and we both laughed. We open the club daily at 3 p.m. for those that need that daily, wind down after work cocktail. I walked up to Joe and the first thing he said was "you look like you've been into something mane." and laughed. I replied "bro it has been a blessed day so far!"I told him Naomi came over. He looked and said "yeah mane I know you had a Great Morning then." We discussed club business, from promotion, drink specials, band Information, all the way down to the lighting improvements. And while we were talking time passed and customers started coming in. Meka and Casey are now behind the bar together and they are taking care of the customers! Tonight is the saxophonist Leroy's night to headline. It's a weeknight but we still expect a nice crowd. They love to hear him blow his sax. Joe and I both have clothes at the club so we wouldn't have to go back home to change for work if we came in a bit early. It's now around 7 p.m. and patrons are steadily coming through the doors and Joe and I are right there greeting them and having small talk to make sure they are enjoying the atmosphere! Just then my phone rang and it was

Tammy. She told me she was pulling up. I told her cool, that I was going to meet her outside so like the gentleman I am, I could escort her in. She said ok. So I walked out the club, I dapped Big T our security guard up and said "its on." He said "Boss you move fast," "I told him you either keep up with the traffic or you get run over!!" We both laughed. I found Tammy's car and she was standing outside of it. As I am walking towards her she is smiling because I am also. With that smile still on her face,she said "you look like you're happy to see me." I told her "with you looking like you're looking, a blind man would give his life to have you in his sight!"She said "oh you Goldie The Mac Or Somebody?" And we both laughed. She was looking elegant. Red Heels, nice form fitting black dress, and a few pieces of jewelry to set it off. We hugged and it was more of a "I'm gonna let you know I want you hug " rather than a friendly embrace." I let her know I was glad she came. She mentioned not having anything else to do, so she decided to come on out. At that time her phone rang. She looked at it, sighed and said "excuse me, i have to take this."

Chapter 3 Part 7 : Play Your Role 2

She stepped off to the side and took the call, it was about a 3 minute call and hell I wasn't tripping because I was enjoying the view! I was looking and fantasizing in my head about how I wanted to fuck the shit out of her if I ever got the chance to do so. Because she is very sexy! She came back and I asked if everything was ok and she said yes. It was just her guy friend she had told me about when we first met. I said "ok cool, not my area to interject on." And we both laughed after I said that. "Are you ready to go into the club?" I asked "Yes, but..." she stopped mid sentence. "But what?" I asked. "Oh it's nothing" she replied with a laugh. I

said cool and we walked up to the club. After I made sure she was seated comfortably, I left to tell Meka and the waitresses to make sure they take care of this customer the same as before. They said we gotcha Boss. Once I made sure that was handled, I walked through the club to find Joe and also to do my nightly rounds that goes along with running the club. The night is flowing smoothly, the house band is sounding Great! People are dancing and drinking and are seemingly having a great time! Tonight is the night where the band and customers have a friendly competition of "who knows what song this is?" The Band plays a few cords of a song and customers take their chances at guessing the name of the song. That game is going over really well so far. Next, the saxophonist will definitely deliver in his headlining performance. A few hours has passed and from working the club to interacting with Tammy it looks like tonight will end on a high Note. She has had about four drinks and she is dancing and vibing to the
music. I walk to her table and she tells me she will be leaving in a few. I told her to take me with her.

She boldly stated, she had planned to do so. Her table was off to the side of the club, and as I was sitting at the table she grabbed my hand and she guided it under the table. She had her dress pulled up a bit with her legs open and no panties on. She took my hand and placed it on her pussy, and said "play with my pussy right now." I am at work and I know this is not the appropriate behavior of a boss but I had to give her what she wanted. So I rubbed her pussy and when I say she was wet...thats a fuckin' understatement! That honey pot was overflowing with juices! so as I rub it and looking in her eyes, I can see how turned on she is and the erotic sensation she is getting from this moment. It seems we are the only ones in the room at this point and the sounds in the club are just on mute right now. So I slid my finger slowly in her pussy and she squirmed a little, her pussy is sooooo warm on the inside, and I commenced to finger her at a steady pace so it wouldn't be noticeable to others. She is biting her lips and closing her eyes enjoying the moment. I went deeper inside of her with my finger one time and she moaned "oh yes." She told me to hold it there because she was about to cum. And she did just that, and to see her control herself at that moment so no one could tell she was cumming in a room full of people turned me on like a motherfucker! But to our surprise it was a couple sitting and watching us the whole time, and it looked as if they were doing the same. Because after she came, I pulled my hand from under the table and I tasted my finger, and the lady at the other table said "I bet she tastes good huh?" I said "Yeah" With a look that said I would love to find out for myself, she replied "she looks like it". We laughed and Tammy said "thank you." We got up so I could walk Tammy out after she gained her composure. I walked her to the car and

told her to wait for me while I go let Joe know that I am leaving for the night and to handle things in the club. She said ok. I went back in and told him and he said I" knew it was coming." Be safe

brother." I Walked back out to her car to see Tammy had started to have her own self pleasuring moment while waiting on me. She was fingering herself in the front seat and she wasn't playing. She was thrusting her fingers in and out of her pussy with aggression, and rubbing her clit at the same time. I stood at the window and watched, and she knew I was watching.

Chapter 3 Part 8 : Let's Go

She looked up but never stopped her motions. She was steadily fucking herself and rubbing her clit, and I can hear her moaning "oh fuck yeah!" To me it seems she loves spontaneity and exihbitionism and that's something I can get down with.Then her eyes start to roll back in her head as if this is about to be the nut of all nuts. She is jerking and squirming and she says yes, um huh, yes, um huh, I'm cumming oh gawd I'm cumming!!! And she did just that. After she came, she licked her own fingers. She looked at me with a hint of embarrassment, but then I asked her, my place or hers? She said "we can go to your place since it's closer" I told her to follow me. .We make it to my house and go inside. She asked if she could shower real quick to freshen up, I told her sure. As she was in the shower I turned on some music and it was a song entitled "For Me" By Da 13th One". I grabbed a bottle of Jose Cuervo from my bar and a couple of shot glasses. I took a few shots to put an edge on my night since I hadn't drunk much of anything due to work. I stripped down to my boxers and was waiting for her to come out. Music playing I'm still pouring up and she comes out wrapped in one of my towels.I looked at her and she didn't hesitate to drop the towel. Aww mane!! I could tell when she was clothed that she was sexy but mane words can't describe her body. She seemed a little self conscious about her midsection because she had a lil stomach, but that was no biggie for me. I took a mental note of that. She approached me as I was sitting down and she asked "where's my shot?" I poured her one and she turned it up and chugged it. After that she asked whose song that was and I told her and she started slowly grooving to it. She looked up and saw I had a sliding door leading to my backyard which was fenced in. She asked if I had nosey neighbors, I said nah. She said "let's fuck outside." I told her to say no more! It was a warm summer night and I guess she wanted the feeling of the night air on her skin. So I grabbed a blanket and we stepped out back. I led her out and the sounds of the crickets made the night setting feel as if we were camping. I had a picnic table on my patio out back and that would be where we would entertain one another. We stood and looked at the stars for a few moments. She then mentioned how beautiful the stars were, as the stars and the full moon illuminated the sky. I was standing behind her and by this time I'd stripped out of my boxers. I started to kiss on her neck softly and sensually as we stood there. She had her hands on top of my hands as I was Slowly caressing her body. I was rubbing on her stomach slowly (assuring her that part wasn't a problem) and I moved my hands gradually up to her breasts. Gripping firmly on them and enjoying the feeling of her soft perky nipples between my thumb and forefinger, as her hands were gripping her breast right along with mine! Then I stepped back, and I told her to bend over and lean on the picnic table. And she didn't hesitate. When she did her pussy poked out as if it wanted me to talk and have a conversation with it!! So I kneeled and admired her nice round ass and I kissed her ass cheek, she giggled. Then I kissed the other. After that I kissed her pussy and I spread her pussy lips open and started to lick Slowly in between them! She starts to moan, and slowly moves her ass to the motions of my tongue. Her pussy is sooo wet, and I am enjoying the taste of her juices. I spread her pussy lips so i can sink my tongue deeper and gradually fuck her with my tongue. Her moans are getting stronger, and she is saying "ummmm" and telling me she likes that! Then I stand up and I lean down and I spread her ass cheeks as I start to lick her asshole, she says "Oh my!"and asked me how I knew she liked that. I told her I was just taking a chance!! And she moaned saying "you guessed right". I licked her asshole until it was wet as if it was her pussy. She leaned up and turned around and told me she was ready to feel my dick inside her!

Chapter 3 Part 9 : Final Moments

She then positioned herself on the table close to the edge so i could have access to fuck her real good!! She leaned over, raised her leg and spreaded her pussy open wide so I could see nside her. She used her pussy muscles and made it contract as if it was talking to me. And at the same time she was pushing cum from inside her pussy. I had to stick my tongue in once more to catch a taste of the cum as she did that. My dick was throbbing and ready to enter Tammy's wet pussy! The humidity outside was mixing with the heat of our bodies and it was bringing on sweat and making the moment much more intense! So I grabbed my dick and slapped it repeatedly on Tammy's wet pussy, then I slowly slid my dick inside her pussy. She then told me to fuck her as if I was being mean to her, and i asked her is if she was sure that's what she wanted. And as I slowly began stroking inside her she moaned yesssss! So I told her here it comes, I gripped both of her legs by the backside of her thighs and pushed them back so I could get deeper in her pussy. I thrusted my dick relentlessly in her pussy, and she said "oooooo, that's what I'm talking about. Give me more." So I continue to pound her pussy, trying to push my dick up in her stomach. And she is grunting and saying "yes." "You better fuck me." "Keep fucking me daddy", and I do just that, dropping dick in her as her juices flow and wet my nuts. I am working hard, sweat is pouring from my head and body. Then I have her turn over on her back and put her legs straight in the air and I wrapped both my arms around them and held them to my chest so I could have straight access to her pussy. And I continue to punish her the way she wants me to. She is telling me thank you, every time I push dick in her! This is some shit I wouldn't expect from her but i am enjoying every fucking moment of it. I speed up fucking her, still thrusting my dick hard and deep in her. And then I go deep and hold my dick deep in her and she gasps as she was becoming short of breath, and at that moment she starts to grip my dick with her pussy, and she starts to say "oh oh oh, I am about to come on your dick daddy." I thrust as she starts to cum and she is cumming hard. As she starts to cum, I pull out of her pussy and begin to suck on her clit, and it sends her body into shock. Her orgasm is so strong she begins to stutter in her speech saying Shiiiiitttt!! She starts to cum again right after she is done with the first nut. I'm sweating, she is sweating and we both are doing what we enjoy! I stand up and start to jack my dick because I was about to cum! Tammy was laying back and she told me to cum on her stomach, and as soon as she said that, I grunted as my legs started trembling and I started to cum and shot cum on her stomach! She rubbed it in with her hand and she licked it off her fingers!! And she said

Thank You! We were two sweaty, sexually satisfied exhibitionists. I just hope we didn't wake my neighbors!!!!!

Chapter 4 : Climax

My alarm sounded so I could get up and get ready for my work day, it's 5:30 a.m. but I don't have to be at work until 7 a.m.. So I start my usual morning routine, I take a few minutes to gather myself after I open my eyes. Then I say a morning prayer while lieing in bed, giving thanks to my Higher Power for blessing me to wake up and see another day! Then I check my phone for texts, social nedia notifications and emails etc.Then at that moment I remembered that I was on vacation for this week from work! Man Damn, I'm tripping now, thinking "how I could forget that",knowing I have been anticipating this time off for a while. I guess my body is locked in on my routine I have to wake up on normal weekdays to prepare for work. So at this point I lay back down to enjoy this free moment!Hadn't planned much of anything to do on my vacation time due to travel restrictions from the pandemic, Covid-19 aka Da Rona that has been drastically affecting the World! So it's gonna mainly be working out and checking on investments that I have and getting in some much needed rest! I may just hit Montgomery Ala one day and see if I can get with this young lady I have been conversing with for the last few months! We haven't linked yet so this free time maybe a good time to do so! Yeah!!

Change of Plans

I have a membership at a local Gym in the city called Crunch Fitness. That junt be packed and I always get a great workout in there! And on the plus side, alot of sexy ladies be all over the gym,and they are very friendly! So I be on 10 when I go there to workout! Today I am just doing a full body touch up workout to get the blood flowing and the muscles tight. Starting with upper body and then moving to lower body stimulation! I walk in and I see a ex co-worker of mine from a previous job I worked at. And she has a body to cherish mane! She always use to talk about perfecting her body,but I use to tell her ,her body was perfect as it is! But being a man I know women always have parts on their bodies that they want to perfect, and we as men just have to agree to disagree with them (No Matter How Sexy We Think You All Are) . We lock eyes and she smiled so big and bright when she seese. And I smiled also, (We Couldn't See The Smiles Foreal, Because Of Our Masks We Had On, But Our Cheek Bones Told The Story) and I thanked God in my head that I chose to come in to workout this morning.We spoke and walked towards one another and hugged. We knew it was out of the norm right now because of the Corona Virus scare,but we were happy to see one another! She asked what have I been up too and I told her just working and maintaining life! I asked her the same and she said she was doing similar to what I was doing! I asked her was she still at the old job and with a sarcastic sigh she said Hell Yeah! And said I don't even want to talk about that place right now. I said cool. We talked for a few more minutes and then exchanged numbers since she was on her way out. She then said she was going to let me get my workout in before we waste all the time talking. We hugged again and she walked off headed out the entrance of the gym. I told her I will text you later, she said don't text,call. I told her that I will do! Then I thought to myself,my vacation is starting off pretty good so far!!

What's Next!

My workout was complete, and I hit the shower right after I finished! I worked very hard today to get a great burn in! Now it's on to see what the rest of this day has to offer! On my way out of the gym I saw and exchanged a few words with a few of the Gyms regular members that I have became cool with since I have been coming to the gym to workout. It's great to meet Genuine Individuals and be able to share positive conversation,even if it's for a short moment. As I walk out of the Gyms entrance my phone rings, and it is Trina, the female from The "Gump" (Nick Name For Montgomery Ala) that I have been conversing with. I answered and we greeted one another how we normally do, and that's by me saying, 'O Nie' and she replies by saying 'Say That Then'! She asked how was I and what was I up to,I then told her what I was doing and about to do. I also told her I forgot that I was on vacation from work this week and I might come see her if she is free to have a visitor! She responded "Might" and told me "Man You Better Bring That Ass On Down To See Me (In A Jokingly Manner)". We both laughed. She then said when I mentioned that it made her forget what she was calling for. We laughed again. She then said she was going to let me go so I can get back on track with my day,but to keep her informed on when I was coming to see her! I said I will do so, and we hung up! As I'm riding in the car I have the song "Ridin Round" Playing by Artist Da 13th One. That Southern slab ridin music. I am headed home but finally got the chance to call Aesha,my ex co-worker that I saw at the Gym. I called,she answered and said she didn't think I was going to call. I told her I couldn't let this chance pass me by! And out Of the 5 years we've worked together I've been wanting to get at her on another level, but I just kept it work related and co-worker friendly in our conversations. She told me she's not slow and that she'd recognized that a couple years in at the job. She said she was just waiting on me to make the first move. I said well damn, but great things come to those when the time is right! She said true,and she felt no time is better than the present,and she laughed. She asked what's my plans for the day. I told her whatever she has going on I want to be apart of it. She said she was off of work for the day and was just going to chill and watch television, I said cool,I'm down to Netflix and Feel, she said that would be worth it only if you could fill up my open holes! I told her there you go talking all that shit like you use to do at work. She said,Nah not me that was you (She Was Referring To Me) that use to be talking big shit like you can put dick down! I told her hell I only speak truth! She told me it's only air and opportunity and the phone calls between us. I told her to send the address and I'm pulling up!! She texted it before I could get the complete sentence out! I told her I will be at your door in 20 minutes. We hung up,and all I could do Is look down at my dick and say MF you better not let me down now!!

My Chance

I stopped at the store and grabbed me a beer and a couple condoms, both are gonna come in handy! I left my phone in the car and when I returned to the car I saw that I had a message from Aesha. I opened the message and it was a video,captioned "Letting You Know This Is Real", and in the video she was slowly rubbing her pussy as she recorded! And then it hit me that shit was real! It's those times when as a man you think you are about to get some unexpected pussy and it doesn't happen. And then times like these when you get reassured that you are about to get some unexpected pussy!! I love times like these! After watching that video my dick was rock hard,I looked down at that mutherfucker and said "You Better Show Out." I texted her back and told her to keep that same energy, I'm on the way! I made it to her house,parked got out and walked to the door,rung the door bell and low and behold Aesha answers the door completely nude! For 5 years of working with her I wondered daily about how she looked naked, and to finally get that chance to see was more than I'd imagined. She asked me "Is This The Energy You Were Referring to", and I told her the exact amount of it that I was referring to! She grabbed my hand and lead me in as I closed the door behind me. Her Ass was mesmerizing me as I was watching it as we walked in. She lead me straight to her bedroom. I am taking every bit of this moment all in, my focus is on one thing only right now! I Don't know what the other parts of her house looked like and not even worried about it at this moment. We made it to her room and she turned around and it seemed as the atmosphere just elevated a notch to extra sexy. She asked do you like what you see? I told her every inch of it,then she asked now what was are you gonna do with it since you talked so much shit. With not a word said I started undressing, but only made it far as taking my shirt off before I couldn't keep my hands off her any longer. As I was taking my shirt off I caught her admiring my body also,for times like these that's when workouts/exercise comes in handy! Women love a little eye candy also. As the shirt came off,I threw it to the floor and I reached out and pulled her close to me! And As soon as I touched her I felt the softness of her skin. I could tell she takes pride in the way she cares for her body. As I pulled her closer , I took the time to appreciate the softness of her body and caress her and rub slowly up and down her back! And Whispered softly in her ear "your body feels so amazing" she replied "it feels even better on the inside"! As a man and to hear a statement like that heightens your sexual level immediately. I start to slowly kiss her neck while still caressing her in my arms and rubbing her back. I then thought I haven't taken my shorts off yet! I told her hold on one second and let me pull my shorts off. She said no let me assist you. And I told her that would be my pleasure to let you do so. I had on gym shorts so it would be easy sliding them junts off! She started to pull my shorts down slowly,checking out how well I have man-scaped my dick and balls! She the said, oh you got him like Mr. Clean down her I see! I told her that's the only way I keep him. She pulls my shorts completely down to see my thick manhood erect and standing at attention. With its veins so visible as if they wanted to pop out of it. She then says,It looks as if someone is ready to play! She then grabs my dick and starts to slowly rub it, she kneels down and she takes her tongue and licks the tip of my dick where there was a bit of pre-cum. She said yeah he is ready! Then she slowly slides it in her mouth (and her mouth is so warm I might add). And I had to release a moan because her mouth felt sooo good,moist and warm!! I then asked her so this was the go feeling inside that you spoke of? In between taking her mouth to the end of my hard dick and coming back up for air, She said no not even close.

I want More

As she was giving me head she slowed up and asked me if she wanted me to record her would I do it? That caught me off guard, in my mind I'm thinking what would she want to use the video for and or would it come back to haunt me. Then I also realized that I am not in a relationship with anyone and why deprive her of her moment. I told her I would be glad to record her. My phone or hers? She said hers. And assured me that she didn't want my face in the video only my dick! I told her I am cool with that. She stood up and grabbed her phone,set it up in record setting for me,and mane let me say that when the camera came on her soul snatcher mode kicked in!! I can tell she's not camera shy and she's done this before,who am I to judge, I'm enjoying the damn ride mane! As I start to record her she was still standing in front of me,she reached out her left hand and placed my dick in the palm of her left hand. And she slowly let a long line of spit fall from her mouth to where my dick was in the palm or her hand. And she started to slowly stroke it back and forth. She softly asked me how does that feel, and I told her that feels good. She then kneeled back down (still stroking my dick in the process) and used her other hand to join in on the stroking motion. If you could see the look in her eyes the way she was zoned out as she worked her hands up and down my dick and spitting on it simultaneously as she stroked to get it sloppy wet and prepared to enter her mouth. I am doing my best to hold the camera steady and not drop it from the sensation she is sending through my body right now. And she looks up at me and In the camera without saying a word,just a sexy stare as if she was hypnotizing me, herself or whoever else will see this. Then she suddenly but slowly eased her mouth around my dick. And mane the wetness and warmth of her mouth was something she had to be blessed with. She then slowly inhaled the same thing me as she took my dick in, deep to the back of her throat. I suddenly noticed she had no gag reflex, because I know my dick is a nice size. As she went down to the base of my dick she extended her tongue out and licked my balls. To record this shit and feeling it at the same time is making me feel porn starish! And I had to cheer her on, that's the way to get the best results of this wonderful moment! As she sucks I repeatedly tell her blow my mind Aesha, Complimenting her on how wet and warm her mouth is,how fire she is with her hand work as she massages while she sucks. Her mouth is Sloppy with spit and every time she goes up and down the dick is sounds like water splashing. She then goes down the dick and holds my dick in her throat until she gags for air! She even grabs my ass and pulls me deeper in. I am recording this and my knees are trying to buckle on me. She comes off it and catches her breathe,while Smacking her face with the dick. And I am telling her I like that shit,do it again. She goes in again,this time she wants me to fuck her mouth. So camera in one hand (trying to hold it steady as I can) And the back of her head in the other I slowly start to fuck her mouth. Then she mouths to me faster,and I sped up as she asked me to do so. Then she said,she was about to cum,This one is a first for me, for her to cum from giving head she is a special type of sex beast!! She said ohhhh and started rubbing her pussy as I was fucking her mouth, and low and behold I myself was feeling I was about to cum also. I told her I am going to cum with you, I slowed my strokes down ,and started slowly stroking as my nut was coming and she was vigorously rubbing her clit to get her nut to come. The phone is shaking, I am shaking, she's shaking and this moment is amazing! Within the next few minutes,she said I am cumming and she starts to hummm on my dick as she says it! And I tell het I am about to cum she is shaking and jerking but she is also focused on catching my nut in her mouth! She grabs my dick and she starts to suck it faster and double stroke to get my nut out. All I can say is Aww Fuck This Feels Good,she keeps on hand on my dick and grabs my balls with the other and massages them to stimulate my cumming sensation. Then here it comes,I tell her it's cumming she said she wanted to taste it all. My dick is throbbing and she is sucking and squeezing it as I shoot cum in her mouth, she catches it then pulls my dick out and puts the rest of the cum on her lips. And rubs it in with my dick as she smacks her face with it. And she is rubbing on and patting her pussy also. Then she looks up in the camera and says so sexy and seductively,we are not done!!!! To be continued......

Credits

Editing: Tawonna Stancer

Photo Cover: Redd Jones